For Boco — J. L.C.

For Dennis, Gregory, Martin, Michael, the three Thomases, Vincent, Walter and Fred — L.C.

I'm gonna like me
when I jump out of bed,
from my giant big toe

the space in my mouth
where two teeth used to be.

I'm gonna like me
wearing flowers and plaid.
I have my own style.
I don't follow some fad.

I'm gonna like me
when I climb on and wave

as the bus pulls away

and I'm feeling so brave.

I'm gonna like me
when I'm called on to stand.
I know all my letters
like the back of my hand.

I'm gonna like me
when my answer is wrong,
like thinking my ruler
was ten inches long.

'cause just like bananas friends come in a bunch.

I'll twist and I'll stretch

straight up to the sky.

I'm gonna like me
when I fall and get hurt
and mess up my elbows
in pebbles and dirt.

I'm gonna like me when I don't run so fast.

Then they pick teams and I'm chosen last.

I'm gonna like me
when I do the right thing
and return what I found
even when it's a...
RING.

MEDAL OF Bravery

MEDAL OF Intelligence

MEDAL OF Adult Cute

MEDAL OF Suave

I'm gonna like me

when I eat something new

1. Catch 150 to 200 lb. octopus.

3. Cook in large pot on stove top. Season well. Stir now and then.

2. Clean well.

4. Serve with rooster foot salad and snail bread.

even if Grandma makes

octopus stew.

I'm gonna like me
when I make a mistake
and put out the candles
on Dad's birthday cake.

I'm gonna like me
when I open the box
and smile and say "Thanks"
even though I got socks.

I'm gonna like me when I try a new task.

I bring in a plate
before I am asked.

I'm gonna like me

when I clean in a flash

and play with my brother

and take out the trash.

I'm gonna like me
when I cuddle up tight
and know as I'm sleeping
I'm safe and all right.

I'm gonna like me
'cause I'm loved and I know it,
and liking myself
is the best way to show it.

I'm gonna like me.

I already do!

But enough about me—

How about